CITIES AND MOVIES

Guturu Karteek

Kindle Direct Publishing

ISBN-13: 9798698271956
ISBN-10: 1477123456

Cover design by: Art Painter
Library of Congress Control Number: 2018675309
Printed in the United States of America

*To the profession of Architecture and Urban Design,
students, friends and family ...*

CONTENTS

INTRODUCTION

The following book compilation is part of the work done by students of Architecture School of Planning and Architecture, Vijayawada, wherein each chapter is based on a movie/series or a game that released before the year 2014. The movies are not limited to one film industry but spans across Hollywood, Bollywood and Tamil Cinema. The objective here is to describe the layers of city character, people and visuals into which the stories are interwoven. While some depictions are fictional either based on comics and/or mythologies, some creates a whole new world where there are different continents. There are the futuristic visions (of the artists) of present-day cities and cities set in historic periods and some totally imagined futures. Some even take us to other planets set in future where the lifestyle is in complete contrast to that of humans on earth where people deal with consequences of human interventions. The Directors, Producers, Writers, Visual Effects team and all other who have contributed to the creation of these movies have been given the due credit at relevant portions of the compilation.

THE HUNGER GAMES

2012

Director : Gary Ross
Producer : Nina Jacobson, John Kilik
Art Director : John Collins
Creative Director: Balind Sieber

Presented by Roshni Roy

The movie is based on the novel -The Hunger Games. It is the first of quadrillage series which depicts the happenings in and around the fictional state of 'Panem'. Panem is a futuristic take on the present day North America-Canada and the capital city. 'The Capitol' is the metaphorical etymology for New York, located in the western rocky mountains.

The story is set in this dystopian post-apocalyptic future in Panem where citizens between the ages of 12 and 18 have to participate in a TV annual event called the Hunger Games. The participants are asked to fight to the death until one victor remains. After the collapse of modern civilization and before the Dark Days rebellion, 13 districts were brought together under the Capitol's rule, forming the nation Panem. District 13 was then destroyed by the Capitol forces as they rebelled against the ruling party. A stark difference is seen between the remaining 12 districts of Panam state and the residents of the Capitol who are far away from the poverty, enjoying a high standard of living and are technologically advanced. They are indifferent towards the desperate and oppressed people of the 12 districts who often have to serve the rich in more ways than one. For instance, the resources harvested like fish, coal, lumber, crops and gems in the districts are exported to the Capitol. Moreover, the apparent criminals or traitors of the districts are often converted into 'Avoxes' wherein their tongues are removed surgically, rendering them mute.

BATMAN: THE DARK KNIGHT

2008

Director : Christopher Nolan
Producer : Christopher Nolan, Emma Thomas, Charles Roven
Creative Director: Wally Pfister
Visual Effects: Paul J. Franklin
Art Director: Craig Jackson and Simon Lamont

Presented by O.Dinesh Kumar

The city portrayed in the movie is a large metropolitan city in the United States called 'Gotham City'. It serves as the home of billionaire Bruce Wayne, who uses his alter-ego of 'Batman' to protect the city against organized crime. Gotham city is portrayed as a dark and foreboding metropolis full of crime, corruption and a profound sense of urban decline. The movie series is based on the DC comics.

The initial movies were directed by Tim Burton, in his version, the visual artists have based their interpretations on art deco and art nouveau architectural styles, such as the Helsinki Central Railway Station. Some exaggerated characteristics of Gothic style can also be seen like massive multi-tiered flying buttresses on Cathedrals.

The 2008 movie, directed and produced by Christopher Nolan interprets Gotham based on Chicago infrastructure and architecture such as Navy Pier. It is cartographically based on canon DC map of Gotham.

JOHN CARTER

2012

Director : Andrew Stanton
Producer : Jim Morris, Colin Wilson, Lindsey Collins
Art Director: David Allday

Presented by Amal Maria Mani

This fictional story is about the protagonist being sent to the planet Mars (called 'Barsoom') where he meets with different civilizations and aliens: a tribe of 9 feet tall 'Tharks'. Mars is depicted as a barren, rocky and geological landscape. The two main cities depicted on Mar named 'Zodanga' and 'Helium' wage war against each other.
Located in the southwest hemisphere, the city of Zodanga is protected by sentries who patrol within the 75 feet high walls surrounding the city. These walls are fifty feet thick constructed on large It is a mobile city which resembles a walking refinery - greasy, smelly, sooty, made of steel and seems lifeless. The city walks over the planet's surface on hundreds of mechanical legs. The attacking airships are housed at the massive hangar decks.
Zodanga has been rebuilt and redeveloped a numerous time over the various wars. The city is destructive in nature where the habitants are hostile and aggressive and they wage war on Helumites, the Tharks and any other enemies crossing their path.

GAME OF THRONES

2011

Director : David Benioff and D.B. Weiss
Producer : David Benioff & D.B.Weiss
Creative Director: Oral Norrey Ottey
Visual Effects: Rainer Gombos, Juri Stanossek, Sven Martin, Steve Kullback and Jan Fiedler
Art Director: Scott Petts

Presented by Amal Jose

Game of thrones is a TV series which depicts a fictional world called 'Westeros', also referred as the Seven Kingdoms. Its royal capital is King's Landing, situated on the Blackwater River on the spot where Aegon the Conqueror landed to begin his conquest.

The main city is fortified by walls and constantly manned by a city watch, called 'gold cloaks'. The 'gold cloaks' are named after the cloaks they wear. A stark difference is seen between the royal life common folk life. The city's natural landscape is dominated by three hills, named after Aegon and his two sisters. The royal castle, the 'Red Keep' is situated on Aegon's hill. It lies close to the water body. The Red Keep seats the royal court and an Iron Throne of the monarch. The series revolve around this Iron Throne, which is believed to be constructed from the swords of Aegon's defeated enemies. The religious centre in King's Landing is depicted by the 'Great Sept of Baelor' or 'Great Sept'. It is considered to be the holiest sept within the Seven Kingdoms. The common public live in shanty settlements. This part of the city is known as 'Flea Bottom'. It is densely populated with slums having no proper drainage system which leaves the city unsightly, dirty and foul smelling. The series is based on the set of novels written by George R. R. Martin of the same name. He compared King's Landing to medieval Paris or London. The sets of the series recreated the artistically imagined city King's Landing into the ideal city concepts, which in turn made it a very big success.

JODHAA AKBAR

2008

Director : Ashutosh Gowarikar
Producer : Roni Screwwala, Ashutosh Gowarikar
Creative Director: Tanushree Dasgupta
Art Director : Nitin Chandrakant Desai

Presented by Lavanya Padala

This movie is based on an Indian epic love story of Mughal emperor Akbar the Great and Rajput princess Jodha set in 16th century. The story is set in three areas: Fatehpur Sikri, Amer Fort, and the royal tents installed during war. Fatehpur Sikri was Akbar's new capital city where he unified the various artistic traditions and architectural styles that were sensitive to different religions like Hinduism and Islam. The same can be seen in 'chhatris', 'minars' (towers), half domed double portals decorated richly in geometric and arabesque designs. These designs were carved on stone in low relief, cut on plaster, painted or inlaid; for instance, various designs of 'jhumkas' (earrings) seen on the wall of Jodhabai's kitchen. Amer fort in Jaipur was residence of Rajputs built by Maan Singh, Akbar's army general. The fort's architecture is a blend of Hindu and Rajput's elements while the ornamentation is influenced by both Hindu and Muslim manner. Magnificent paintings of hunting scenes on the walls reflect the temperament of the Rajputs, who were daring, revolutionary and self-indulgent. The royal tents or the movable cities were set up for campaigning done by rulers for either war, peace or an alliance. A plain look from outside, the inside is decorated with patterned and embroidered fabrics. The tents had semi-public spaces that created a royal look as that of a palace.

WALL E

2008

Director: Andrew Stanton
Producer : Jim Morris
Creative Director: Martin Rosenberg
Visual Effects: Juan J. Vuhler
Art Director: Anthony Christov, Jason Dreamer

Presented by C. Manikanteswara

It is a science fiction film portraying romance between two robots - Wall-E and Eve, programmed for different works in different worlds. The movie addresses consumerism, nostalgia, environmental problems, waste management, the immense impact humans have on the planet Earth, and risks to human civilization.

In 2105 A.D. the earth is filled with debris and the home planet is abandoned. The population is evicted in starliner spacecrafts built by Buy 'n' Large. One of the spacecrafts is Axiom which is an extra-terrestrial city. The Earth is left with a few auto-bots, programmed to gather the garbage and pile it as building blocks. The city of Axiom resembles Dubai and Shanghai while the artificial lighting of the city resembles the Las Vegas. The design of the city is inspired from the Santiago Calatrava's futuristic architecture. The city is divided into three sections: economy class, coach class, and the premier class. All the sections are differentiated by the types of spaces, material textures and graphic colours. Axiom is completely mechanized, where people do not feel the beauty of the city as they float in their seats in a queue for travelling. For longer distances a rapid transit system is used.

The commercial area and gathering spaces, located at the centre of the city are colourful and well lit. It circumscribes a transit circular expressway. The public spaces are pictures as non-interactive but individually enjoyable spaces. Despite being futuristic and bright, the city is not emotionally felt by the citizens, thus feeling nostalgic after living there for 700 years.

UPSIDE DOWN

2012

Director : Juan Diego Solanas
Producer : Onyx Films Studio 37
Art Director: Jean Pierre Paquet, Isabelle Guay

Presented by Aflah Ahammed

The movie portrays a fictional 'two-planet home world', which is different from any other planetary system because it has 'dual-gravity'. The phenomenon of dual gravity helps the two planets to orbit around each other in close vicinity. The planet system follows three laws of gravity: all matter is drawn by the gravity of the world from which it originates and not from the other; second, all objects weight can be offset using matter from the opposite world (inverse world); and third, within a few hours of contact, matter in contact with inverse matter, burns.

The exception of the laws can be seen in headquarters of the 'trans world' company where there is a physical connection linking the worlds. Working spaces for people of both worlds are together, where the spaces have double room heights. Ceiling of one world is the flooring for the other.

City planning is differentiated between the two worlds with respect to the functions and economies of the worlds. Both are segregated by the law. The upper world is rich and prosperous. The lower world is poor. The rich buy cheap oil from the poor and sell back electricity at a higher price, while dumping all the waste in the lower world.

ELYSIUM

2013

Director : Neil Blomkamp
Producer : Bill Block, Neil Blomkamp
Art Director : Don Macaulay
Creative Director: Phillip Ivey

Presented by G.Nikhila

Elysium is an American dystopian, action and thriller movie which is set in the year 2154 taking place on a ravaged Earth and a space habitat, Elysium. The story revolves around political and sociological issues involving immigration, overpopulation, health care, exploitation and class issues.

The Earth dwellers feel trapped in the giant planet-bound slum. Their collective dream is to live in Elysium - the orbiting space colony with clean breathable air, clear streams and rivers, crime free streets. They dream of using Elysium's medical technology wherein full body scanners eradicate disease and reverse decay but Elysium is a gated community which only houses wealthy citizens.

Elysium's design depicts pastoral landscapes wrapped inside a toroidal structure curving upwards as far as the eye can see. It is peppered with low density, campus style architecture, discreet hi-tech and healthy-looking citizens. Many built structures and views seen in the movie exists today, like a villa in Milan; Santiago Calatrava's City of Arts and Sciences in Valencia - depicted as Elysium's Amrine Opera House. Also, the space views are inspired

GUTURU KARTEEK

from the NASA archives.

TOTAL RECALL

2012

Director : Len Wiseman
Producer : Toby Jaffe
Art Director: Oana Bogdan Miller

Presented by G. Dyaneshwar

The fictional film is based on the book "We Can Remember it for you wholesale" where the author depicts the future of the planet Earth, predicting the devastation of Earth by chemical warfare at the end of the 21st century. The small amount of remaining habitable land is then divided into two territories: The United Federation of Britain (UFB) and the Colony (Australia). Colony residents travel to the UFB to work in factories through a gravity elevator, 'the fall' that runs through the Earth's core.

The infrastructure depicted is developed vertically due to lack of space on the surface. The future is technologically advanced, retaining a level of level of plausibility in the designed world. Here, the architecture is a blend of modern and neoclassical styles. It is a multi-level environment where buildings are built above or hanging under huge platforms stacked in complex arrangement making the environment busy and cohesive. The lack of green spaces, flora and fauna is clearly visible. In this future depiction, the transportation systems include "hover cars" that run on bridges connecting the taller structures and also an underground transit involving capsules that run along the cables.

THE FIFTH ELEMENT

1997

Director : Luc Besson
Producer : Patrice Ledou
Creative Director : Ricky Nierva
Art Director : Ron Gress, Ira Gilford
Visual Effects: Ron Gress

Presented by Pranjal Gupta

The movie is set in the futuristic imagination of the New York city, 250 years from now in the 23rd century. The city portrayed has existing structures with new additions both at the top and bottom. In this new version, the city's circulation is vertical rather than horizontal which is made possible by slicing it into vertical canyons. So, instead of road transportation, people in 23rd century use 'hovercrafts'. As the plane of the city shifted from horizontal to vertical, the underground structures including the city's utilities were exposed, metro system got integrated vertically. The overall appearance is industrial and machine-like. The movie depicts the antagonist, Zorg's powerful status through the elements of architecture. Zorg's residence is one of the tallest building in the city with powerful portray of capitalism. In the year 2259, New York becomes the capital of the world and is a part of the colonized solar system. The population of the city increased to 200 billion and due to scarcity of land, the city keeps on developing vertically. A dwelling unit is shown as compact as possible, just a single room in which the kitchen, the bath as well as the bedroom is present. All the equipments are movable and focus on the comfort of the person residing.

MAFIA II

2010

Game Developer: 2K Czech, Massive Bear Studios, Feral Interactive
Producer : 2K games, 1C Company, Feral Interactive, Connect2Media
Designers: Daniel Vavra, Pavel Brzak

Presented by Oded Darlong

The storyline of the game is based upon a 1940-60 war hero Vito Scaletta, in the winter of 1945. The city of Empire Bay is divided into two parts by the river passing through. The game exists in 2 time periods: the 1940s and 1960s, where the hero is released from jail after 5 years of imprisonment.

In the 1940s, the city is under development and sparsely populated. The urban characteristics seen here are: open spaces like empty plots, open air restaurants; old residential houses with wood construction; roads without pavements making it pedestrian unfriendly.

In the 1960s, the same city is depicted as developed in terms of infrastructure. The urban characteristics seen here are: high rise buildings; flyovers and bridges made in steel and concrete, connecting the two parts of the city. The city is planned by enhancing the quality of spaces as seen through landscape and road connectivity.

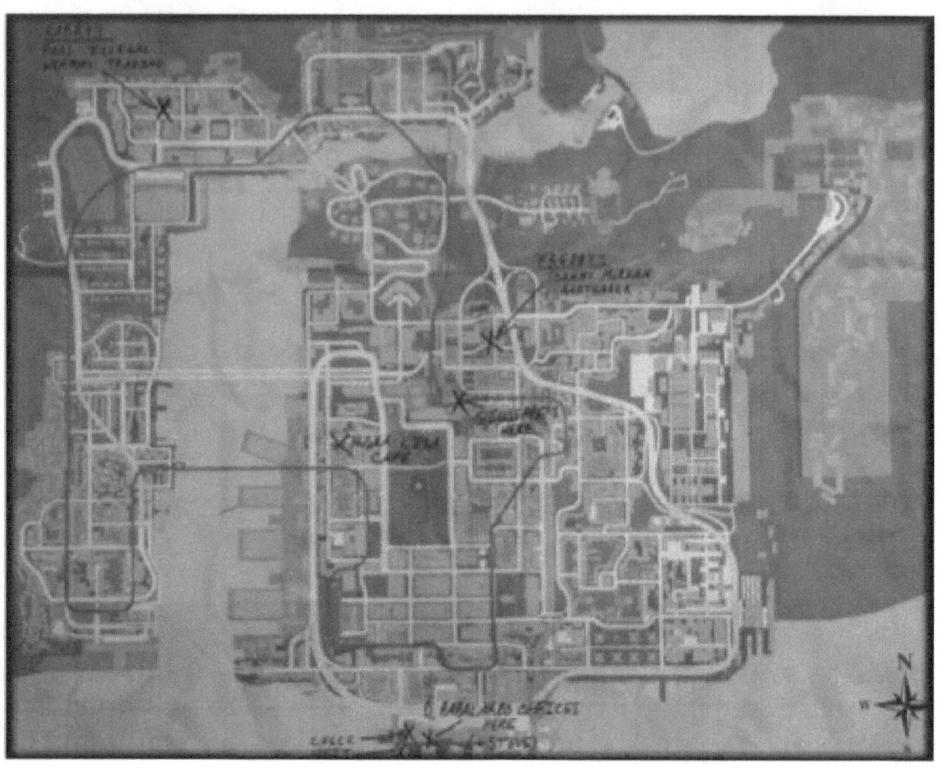

SHERLOCK HOLMES

2012

Director : Guy Ritchie
Producer : Joel Silver, Lionel Wigram
Creative Director : Danny Yount
Art Director : Davyd Shurmer
Visual Effects: Lucy Ainsworth Taylor

Presented by R. Satish

The movie is set in the period 1870-1920 in the city of London when it achieved its final transformation as one of the Urbanized Capitals of the world. It underwent a major change in parts of economics, industrial, political as well as poverty. It hedged along with New York to be dominant city of the world.

In the early 19th century, London became a financial city with the industrial revolution, where previously it was an agricultural city. It became highly populated and the city started developing in areas of transportation, postal communication, and architecture. Representation in the movie is in accordance with the time period and the extension to which London's situation being portrayed. The cityscape depicted in the movie includes the beginnings of modern architectural structures, steam engines as a public transport and development of sewer systems throughout London. Within the span of 50 years, the population escalated from 1 million to 6.7 million mostly because of immigrants. Great Britain became the biggest colonial power of that time, giving access to various technologies, investment and labour from many countries. This added to the socio-economic status of the city. The movie promoted this development all along, including the establishment of the Royal Academy of Science and construction of the London Bridge.

STAR TREK INTO DARKNESS

2013

Director : J.J.Abrams
Producer : J.J.Abrams, Bryan Burk, Damon Lindelof, Alex Kurtzman
Creative Director: Roberto Orci, Alex Kurtzman, Daniel Mindel
Visual Effects: William Morrison, Russell Mc Coy, Darell Abney
Art Director: Ramsey Avery, Kasra Farahani

Presented by Abhishek M.

Second in the movie series, Star Trek into Darkness is an action and fiction film which depicts future version of London and San Francisco in the year 2259. The visual artists not only created brand new urban landscapes from scratch, they re-engineered the existing ones. The concrete facades seen in the movie look as if they've made a comeback in the 2200s; some buildings going up to 200 stories tall. The artists have not arbitrarily portrayed the gleaming towers of a galvanized skyline that is by far the trend in portraying futuristic cities in fiction. They analysed the historic growth of London in the last 100 years, confirming the existence of many old buildings even after centuries. In doing so the city model that was developed seemed real with scalable architecture. Further, modern city with more smog is what people usually expect futuristic cities to look like now.

GUTURU KARTEEK

THOR: THE DARK WORLD

2013

Director : Alan Taylor
Producer :Kevin Feige
Art Director: Julian Ashby, thomas Brown
Set Decoration: John Bush

Presented by Pradeep Kumar

Produced by Marvel Studios, Thor: The Dark World is an American superhero film featuring the Marvel Comics character Thor. The city 'Asgard' depicted in this movie is drawn from Norse Mythology. Asgard is one of the nine worlds mentioned realms in Norse Mythology, where Earth is named Midgard.It is the home to a group of powerful beings including Thor, considered as Gods by humans. It is different from planetary bodies in the earth dimension by not being a sphere, but rather a flat landmass of a small city suspended in space. Asgard's gravity is similar to that of Earth's and the common matter like rocks, water, steel, flesh and bones is denser, thus more durable. The King's palace or tower is situated in the centre of the city, surrounded by the common people. The city's infrastructure spans both vertically and horizontally. The buildings have their individual design which holds traces of Greek architecture like columns to showcase the power of Asgard by placing it alongside the entry of the King's palace. The buildings in the central part of the city are shown to be made up in gold where the texture is used to showcase the love for antiques. There is a bridge that connects Asgard and Bifrost, a link between all the nine worlds. The texture of the bridge seems rainbow-like and is very powerful which would destroy the link between the worlds if left unguarded.

THE SIMPSONS MOVIE

2007

Director : David Silverman
Producer : James L.Brooks, Matt Groening, Al Jean, Mike Scully, Richard Sakai
Art Director : Dima malanitchev

Presented by D.Lakshmi Varshini

This movie is a 2007 American animated comedy based on the TV series-The Simpsons. The movie is set in a fictional mid-sized town - Springfield in United States. The town's geography is varied which includes forests, meadows, mountain ranges, a desert, a gorge, a glacier, beaches, Badlands, canyons, swamps, a harbour, waterholes and waterways. Moreover, there is a portal to another dimension in a place called Springfield Mystery Spot. Springfield is portrayed as a self-sustained town. The town has several universities, museums, churches and concert halls. Springfield is equipped with an international airport, railroad and a public transit system. The streets of the city are maintained with appropriate street furniture and services. The issue faced by the people of the city was an unusually polluted environment. The old town became a massive dump because of the overflowing garbage which forced the whole town to move 8 km away. Moreover, the town has a hazardous waste treatment centre that sends the waste into the river, even dumping the dead bodies inside. Though the movie focuses on this issue, in the end the community collectively gather to clean the river.

MIDNIGHT IN PARIS

2011

Director : Woody Allen
Producer : Letty Aronson, Stephen Tenenbaum, Jaume Roures
Art Director : Darius Khondji
Creative Director: jean Yves Rabier

Presented by Manish Paul Simon

The movie is set in Paris where the city is shown through the protagonist, Gil's eyes. Gil is a writer who explores the city to get new ideas for his book. The exploration reveals various architecture styles.

The movie is set in several time periods and Paris glows intensely and seductively in every one of those. It is visible through the visual artist's recreation of older time periods with landmarks, architectural details, reflective streets. Le Grand Vefour, now a restaurant was a cafe opened in 1784 as depicted in the movie. Another place showcased is Quai De la Toumelle, a walkway bordering the bank of the river Seine. It attracts the students and couples alike along with being a popular filming location. A bridge called Pont Alexandre III, as shown in the movie is an Art Nouveau representation of the 1892 alliance between Russia and France. It connects the Champs - Elysees to the Eiffel Tower.

UNDER THE TUSCAN SUN

2003

Director : Audrey Wells
Producer : Tom Sternberg
Art Director : Edigio Spugnini
Creative Director: Gian Franco Fumagelli

Presented by Navyusha Pentakota

The movie is set in the Tuscany region of Italy showcasing various cities and towns like Florence (capital city), Montepulciano, Cortona and Arezzo. These places represent Tuscan-Gothic style of architecture. The prevailing character of Florence architecture is medieval with steep narrow streets situated on the hillside.

The towns were built on the hills as a defensive manoeuvre for their earliest inhabitants, fortified with thick walls and steep embankments.

Research shows that the earthworks, stone and wooden Palisades were replaced by stone and masonry walls, stronger gates and watchtowers in the middle ages. These historic structures often survive earthquakes that destroy the modern buildings in the same vicinity. Further the movie displays a typology of open spaces that depicts the hierarchy of spaces, open pockets, courtyards sporting flower decked walls, alleys that dead end into red tiled roof top panoramas. The common spaces include Siena's central piazza which invites people with its gently tilted floor fanning out from the city hall tower. It is a vehicular free zone. The church facades are intricately ornamented which shows the Baroque style.

42

THE MATRIX TRILOGY, ANIMATRIX

2003

Director : The Wachowsky Brothers
Producer : Joel Silver
Visual Effects: John Gaeta
Creative Director: Balind Sieber

Presented by Sravan Sateesh

Zion is a fictional city depicted in the movie series 'Matrix' which is considered as the last human inhabited area on earth with a population of 2.5 lakhs. In the movie, an after-war situation is portrayed wherein the humans lost to their own creation of machines. As a last resort, the humans then blocked the machines' main energy source, i.e. the sun by creating a smoke shield over the atmosphere.

To survive, the machines constructed a place called Matrix where they kept captured humans and used their brain's biochemical energy as an alternative energy source by connecting their minds to this imaginary world. This will keep their brains functional and hence the machines get an infinite renewable energy source.

Zion was built by the humans who were not captured or who escaped the Matrix. It is an underground city situated 4 km deep below the earth's surface, above the mantle. The city is divided into 8 levels according to different functions.

MADRASAPATTINAM

2010

Director : A.L.Vijay
Producer : Kalapathi S. Aghoram
Creative Director: Nirav Shah
Visual Effects: Karthik Kotamraju
Art Director: Selva Kumar

Presented by Aflah Ahammed

It is a love story portrayed in the 1940s in Madras (now Chennai) when the Britishers were about to leave India. The recreation of the city done by the art director displays the right look as was at that time, for instance the characteristics of the 'dhobi khana', the Central Station, trams, waterways at Buckingham canal used for ferrying, the government houses, crowded marketplaces and narrow streets. Moreover, the lights and shades, colour tones and textures seem research based.

Chennai is home to the largest collection of heritage buildings in the country, which is evident in the movie itself. The architecture style includes Pallava style, chola style, Vijayanagara empire style and Indo - Saracenic style.

GUTURU KARTEEK

TROY

2004

Director : Wolfgang Peterson
Producer : Wolfgang Peterson
Art Director : Julian Ashby, Jon Billington, Stephen Dobric

Presented by Nadir Noori

Troy is an epic war movie based on Homer's Iliad (ancient Greek epic poem) which talks about the Trojan War that went on for 10 years and revolves around the warrior Achilles who led the Greek army to invade the historical city of Troy. As depicted in the movie, the city was constructed on a hill and its down area. It had natural defensive systems in the form of mountains surrounding three of the sides. Along with this, the city had strong fort walls built with watch towers and only one gate at the front side facing the sea. The city was divided into two parts: citadel, located on the elevated part which was separated by walls from the lower part and the town for common people. The Troy fort was situated 20 km from the sea shore and all buildings were inside the city except for a few watch towers. The infrastructure of the entire city including the palace show uniform construction style with sandstone and wood being the common construction material. The buildings have heights varying from 5 to 20 meters, though the watch towers had a height of more than 20 meters. Temples and official buildings like armoires can be recognised by their high plinth levels of about 2.5 meters height and huge pillars. The main road leading from the fort gate to the palace was about 10 m wide passing through the city centre, a square shaped gathering space surrounded on three sides by temple of Greek gods like Zeus, Apollo and Athena. Along with social activities like celebrations, burials and quick army formations, commercial activities were also concentrated in and around this area. The city of Troy was destroyed by the enemy forces, but as it was built with strong materials there is still evidence of its existence in present day Turkey.

MONSTERS UNIVERSITY

2013

Director : Dan Scanlon
Producer : Kori Rae
Creative Director : Ricky Nierva
Art Director : Robert Kondo
Visual Effects: Joshua Jenny

Presented by Kuldeep Mathur

The movie is set in the fictional world of monsters taking place at a 'scare school', Monsters University. The uniqueness in designing such a school comes with accommodating monsters of different heights, flying monsters, underwater monsters, heavier monsters. This is incorporated in facilities like water fountain which is multileveled, catering to both short and tall monsters. Moreover, the staircase has steps within steps that allow two scales of the monsters to climb. Flying monsters have a separate wing - the aviation wing with perches at the top floor for landing. Underwater monsters have a part of campus to themselves which is submerged in the river. For heavier monsters, a weighted trapezoid element is added from the university's gates to the hostel interiors. The visual artists created this university with a history. The oldest part of the campus is in the region of the fountain statue of the founder. Here the well-worn paths are visible, also pathways with cobblestones are only found in this part of the campus. The structures are built with monstrous details like spikes, horns, tentacles, fangs all over along with the the vegetation creeping across on the tentacles across the buildings.

ACKNOWLEDGEMENT

I would like to thank all the students who have worked on the compilation of this academic exercise as part of the Urban Design Elective subject in Bachelors of Architecture namely Dinesh Kumar, M.Abhishek, K.Giridhar, C.Manikanteswara, Aflah Ahammed, Dyaneshwar, Amal Maria Mani, Oded Darlong, Pradeep Kumar, Lavanya Padala, N.Lohita, Manish Paul Simon, Sai Mrudula, P.Navyusha, G.Nikhila, Roshni Roy, Sravan Sateesh, Nadir, Lakshmi Varshini, K.Sidharth, Kuldeep Mathur, Pranjal Gupta, Sameer Ali and R.Satish. I thank Himani Goel (Student of Masters of Architecture) for putting the additional effort in finalising the last cut of the compilation and co-editing the compilation. I wish to thank the Institute and the Department for supporting this compilation.

ABOUT THE AUTHOR

Guturu Karteek

 G.Karteek is an Architect and Urban Designer from India. He finished his Masters in Urban Design from School of Planning and Architecture, New Delhi and presently working as an Assistant Professor in School of Planning and Architecture Vijayawada (SPAV) since 2009. He was the recipient of the Erasmus Plus Global Mobility Scholarship to visit Norwegian University of Science and Technology (NTNU), Trondheim, Norway and was also part of the European Union funded project Building Resilient Urban Communities (BReUCom) in partnership with Krems University, Austria. His academic contributions include authoring several research papers, organizing several workshops, special lectures and events related to Architecture and Urban Design. His current research is on Floor space Index and Liveability of residential neighborhoods in the Indian context.

9 798698 271956